For Samuel:
It's all in your imagination.

—R.M.

For Lukie

—L.B.

Did You Say
GHOSTS?

by Richard Michelson
illustrated by Leonard Baskin

Macmillan Publishing Company   New York
Maxwell Macmillan Canada   Toronto
Maxwell Macmillan International   New York   Oxford   Singapore   Sydney

Library of Congress Cataloging-in-Publication Data
Michelson, Richard. Did you say ghosts? / by Richard Michelson ; illustrated by Leonard Baskin. — 1st ed.   p.   cm. Summary: A parent's teasing assurances that ghosts, witches, vampires, and other creatures are no danger fuel the imagination of a child in the dark. ISBN 0-02-766915-7 [1. Monsters—Fiction. 2. Fear—Fiction. 3. Bedtime—Fiction. 4. Night—Fiction. 5. Stories in rhyme.] I. Baskin, Leonard, ill. II. Title. PZ8.3.M5718Di 1993 [E]—dc20   92-30134

For the last time

                       turn off the light

and go to sleep.

                  It's late at night.

Everything will be all right.
There aren't any ghosts in sight.
It's all in your imagination.

GHOSTS!
DID YOU SAY GHOSTS?

There's no such thing as spooks or ghosts.
I guarantee it...well, almost.

And if there were, the werewolves' bay—
AIYAAAAAAAAAAAAAAAY—
would scare even a ghost away.

WEREWOLVES!
DID YOU SAY WEREWOLVES?

I'm only kidding, silly child.
You'd think we lived out in the wild.

Don't worry. Even if a bite
could turn kids into wolves at night,
I'll protect you. Anyway,
giants will scare the wolves away.

GIANTS!
DID YOU SAY GIANTS?

Most giants I know, all in all,
would rather be sharp-witted, small
and quick,
        than slow,
                and dumb,
                      and tall.

I've seen a tiny demon frighten
the biggest mean and hungry titan.

DEMONS!
DID YOU SAY DEMONS?

Quiet down and stop that screaming.
You should be asleep and dreaming.

I made it up. It isn't true.
Demons are twice as scared as you
of being caught and dropped into
a wicked witch's boiling brew.

WITCHES!
DID YOU SAY WITCHES?

Relax. There's not a thing to fear.
You'll never find a broomstick here.

If I were you I'd bet my britches
that vampires can scare those witches.

VAMPIRES!
DID YOU SAY VAMPIRES?

Bloodsucking fangs...there's no such thing.
I'm fooling you. Stop fidgeting.
Even a count with black bat wings

would, if he woke, be scared to death
of a dragon's fiery breath.

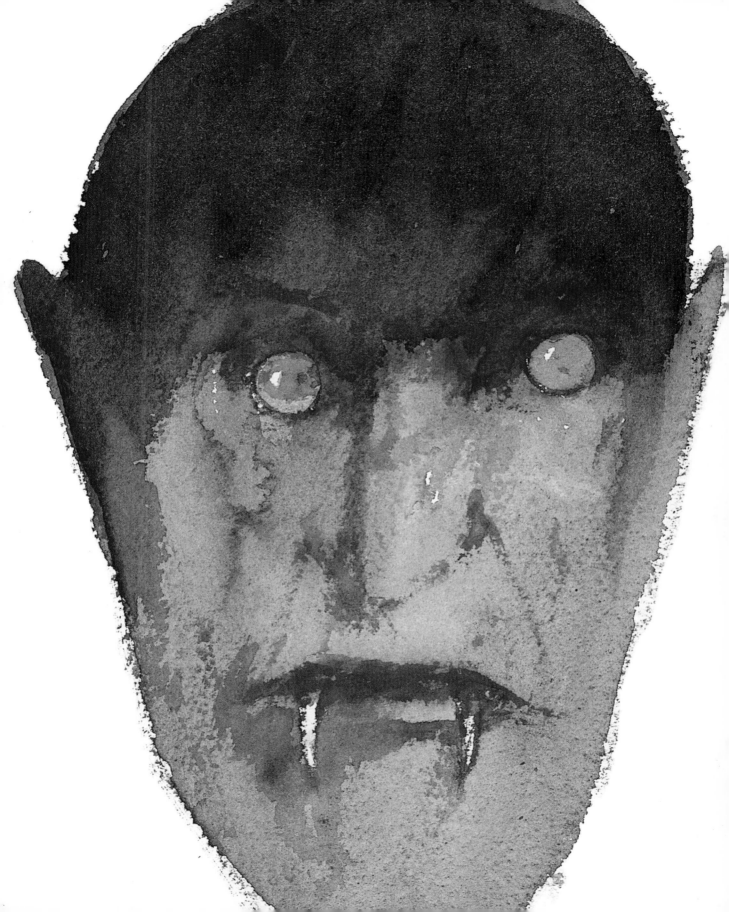

DRAGONS!
DID YOU SAY DRAGONS?

You're draggin' this on, on, and on.
If dragons lived, their time's long gone.

And even if one did survive,
gargoyles eat dragons alive.

GARGOYLES!
DID YOU SAY GARGOYLES?

Covered head to toe with boils,
warts, and scaly snakeskin coils,

gargoyles wait till you're alone
and then they spring to life full grown.
But any gorgon, it's well known,
can turn a gargoyle into stone.

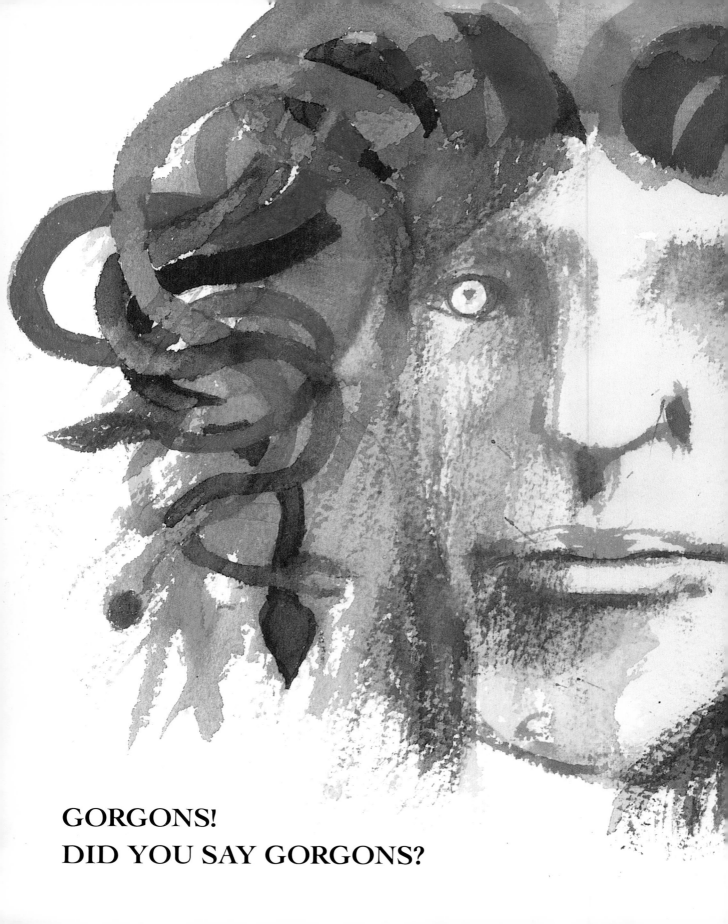

GORGONS!
DID YOU SAY GORGONS?

I didn't mean to cause a scare.
No one has snakes instead of hair.
It's myth. Now say a good-night prayer
and let your eyes close...

                                if you dare.

Besides, those gorgons stay away
when skeletons come out to play.

SKELETONS!
DID YOU SAY SKELETONS?

Everyone I've ever known
needs blood and guts and skin. Just bone
can't possibly live on alone.

But if old bones could dance at night,
ghouls would chase them out of sight.

GHOULS!
DID YOU SAY GHOULS?

I'm only joking. Don't be fooled.
No one has ever seen a ghoul
that ate dead flesh, robbed graves, or drooled.
I promise. You can ask at school.

Ghouls hide in closets, cupboards, stoves,
because they're scared of slithy toves.

SLITHY TOVES!
DID YOU SAY SLITHY TOVES?

Toves are all your own creation.
They grow in your imagination.

Now go to sleep.
    Turn off the light.
There's not a slithy tove in sight.

And if one does appear tonight,
every child...well, almost,

knows slithy toves are scared of ghosts.

GHOSTS!
DID YOU SAY GHOSTS?